D0018740

The Homesick Puppy

Pet Rescue Adventures:

Max the Missing Puppy

Ginger the Stray Kitten

Buttons the Runaway Puppy

The Frightened Kitten

Jessie the Lonely Puppy

The Kitten Nobody Wanted

Harry the Homeless Puppy

Lost in the Snow

Leo All Alone

The Brave Kitten

The Secret Puppy

Sky the Unwanted Kitten

Misty the Abandoned Kitten

The Scruffy Puppy

The Lost Puppy

The Missing Kitten

The Secret Kitten

The Rescued Puppy

Sammy the Shy Kitten

The Tiniest Puppy

Alone in the Night

Lost in the Storm

Teddy in Trouble

A Home for Sandy

The Homeless Kitten

The Curious Kitten

The Sad Puppy

The Abandoned Puppy

A Kitten Named Tiger

The Forgotten Puppy

The Stolen Kitten

Also by Holly Webb:

Little Puppy Lost

The Homesick Puppy

ROWLETT PUBLIC LIBRARY
3900 MAIN STREET
ROWLETT, TX 75088
WITHDRAWN

by Holly Webb

Illustrated by Sophy Williams

tiger tales

tiger tales

5 River Road, Suite 128, Wilton, CT 06897
Published in the United States 2018
Originally published in Great Britain 2007
as *Ellie the Homesick Puppy* by the Little Tiger Group
Text copyright © 2007 Holly Webb
Illustrations copyright © 2007 Sophy Williams
ISBN-13: 978-1-68010-431-8
ISBN-10: 1-68010-431-4
Printed in China
STP/1800/0181/0218
All rights reserved
10 9 8 7 6 5 4 3 2 1

For more insight and activities, visit us at www.tigertalesbooks.com

Contents

Chapter One
Packing Up 7

Chapter Two
In the Way 26

Chapter Three
A Confusing Change 35

Chapter Four
Escaping Grandma's 57

Chapter Five
On the Run! 76

Chapter Six
Homeward Bound 97

Chapter Seven
Solving the Puzzle 107

Chapter Eight
Home at Last 117

For Tom, Robin, and William

Chapter One
Packing Up

"Megan, you're supposed to be packing those books, not reading them!"

Megan looked up guiltily at her mom.

"I'm sorry! I found this one under my bed, and I'd forgotten I even had it. I haven't read it in a long time." Megan reluctantly put the book inside a box and sighed.

Mom smiled. "Oh, go ahead, you can

keep it out—we've got a couple more days until we go anyway. You'll go crazy without a book to read."

Megan nodded and laid the book on her pillow as Mom headed back downstairs. She sat down on her bed and shook her head disbelievingly.

"A couple more days, Kiki. Only two more nights sleeping in this bedroom," she muttered.

Kiki clambered up onto Megan's knee, wagging her tail, and then licked her hand lovingly. She didn't know why Megan sounded worried, but she wanted to help.

"You're excited too, aren't you?" Megan said, smiling. "You don't have to go to a new school, though, lucky Kiki." She petted Kiki's golden ears, and

the little puppy shivered with delight.
Then she curled up on the comforter
again, working herself into a little
yellow furry ball.

Moving to a new house was exciting and scary at the same time. Megan's bedroom there was much bigger than this one, which would be great—but then she was really going to miss her best friend, Taylor, and all her friends at school. They had finished for the Easter vacation the day before, and everyone in her class had gotten together to make her a huge card, with all their photos on it and a message from each of them. She'd almost cried when they gave it to her, thinking how they'd all tried so hard to make it special. It was sitting on her desk now, so she could pack it very carefully at the top of one of the boxes, last thing. Megan looked at it and sighed.

It wasn't as if they were actually

moving all that far—only about 10 miles; it wasn't the other side of the country, or anything like that. But it meant a new school, of course, and a whole bunch of new people. *New friends*, Megan told herself firmly.

The best thing was that in two days' time, Megan and Kiki would be able to step out of their back door and explore wherever they wanted. Here they only had the park, and Megan wasn't allowed to walk Kiki on her own. She knew she was going to have to be very careful going for walks in the countryside near their new house, and every time she mentioned it, Mom kept reminding her about being responsible and not going too far. But all the same, she was practically going to have a forest at the end of her yard! It was going to be wonderful! She'd be able to take Kiki over to her grandma's house, too, since Grandma lived within walking distance of their new house.

Megan gently petted Kiki's soft golden back, and the little dog gave a sleepy whine and half rolled over, inviting Megan to rub her tummy. She yawned a huge yawn, showing her very white teeth, and opened her eyes, blinking lovingly up at Megan.

Megan smiled back at her. "I just can't wait to take you for walks in those woods," she whispered happily. "It's going to be the best thing ever!"

Kiki sprang up and gave an excited, hopeful little bark.

Megan laughed. "You heard me say the W word, didn't you, Kiki-pie? I can't believe you want to go out again. We've only been back home an hour!"

Kiki was wagging her tail like crazy now, staring up at Megan, but Megan shook her head.

"I'm sorry, Kiki. Mom says I have to pack."

Kiki didn't understand exactly what Megan was saying, but she knew what that tone of voice meant. No walk. She lay back down on the bed, her head resting mournfully on her paws. She knew they'd had a long walk, but now that she'd had a little nap, she felt like going out for another run.

Megan laughed at her. "You're such an actress, Kiki! You're behaving like I never take you for walks. And it's not fair, because you know I'd love to. But we have to get everything into boxes." She sighed. "And Mom's only given me these. She says if I can't get all my stuff in here, I'm going to have to sort some of it out and get rid of it." She looked around her room worriedly. It seemed like an awful lot to fit into such a small stack of boxes.

Megan went over to the windowsill and started to pack her collection of toy dogs into a box. She had so many, all different breeds, but more than half of them were Labradors, like Kiki. Officially, she was a yellow Labrador, but Megan thought yellow wasn't the right word at all. Kiki was really a rich honey-golden color, with pale cream fur on her tummy. Her ears were a shade darker than everywhere else, and super-silky. Mom thought that Kiki might get darker as she got older, to match her ears, but Megan wasn't sure. She would be growing for a while still, anyway; she was just four months old at the moment. But even though Kiki was only a puppy, she was always bursting with energy.

Kiki stared soulfully at Megan, watching her tape up the box. It looked fun. Her ears twitched, and her tail wagged a little. Maybe she could jump at that tape! She was never quite sure what was naughty, and sometimes jumping at things got her in trouble....

Suddenly, Kiki's ears pricked up. She could hear someone coming down the driveway. Tail wagging, she stood up on the bed to look out the window, and gave Megan a little warning bark. It was Taylor!

Before Taylor even had the chance to ring the bell, Megan and Kiki raced out of the room and down the stairs, heading for the front door. Kiki won easily. She always did. She was amazingly fast. She scratched at the front door with her paws, barking excitedly, until Megan caught up.

"Shhh! Kiki, shhh! Come back! I can't open the door when you've got your paws on it, can I?"

Kiki scampered back, panting excitedly. She knew Megan's friend Taylor, and she hoped this meant a walk after all. She was used to walking with

Taylor, as Megan and her mom usually picked Taylor up on the way to school. Kiki and Megan often walked around the corner to Taylor's house when they went to the park, too, since Megan's parents didn't like her going on her own, even when she had Kiki with her.

"Hi, Megan! Mom said I could come over and help you pack, if that's okay with your mom and dad." Taylor looked hopefully at Megan's dad, who was struggling into the hall carrying a huge box of china from the kitchen.

"Umph! Fine by me," Dad said, putting down the box carefully. "But make sure you *do* pack, girls, okay? Not just chatting."

Taylor looked around Megan's room. "All these boxes!" She slumped down on Megan's bed sadly, and Kiki scrambled up after her to lick her face. "Oof, not so much, Kiki! Oh, Megan, I've known for a long time you were going, but it seems so real now."

Megan sat down beside her, and Kiki wriggled happily between them. "I know. Packing makes it seem as though it really is happening. The day after tomorrow...." Megan's voice wobbled, and Kiki turned to lick her, too. What was the matter with them? She looked worriedly from Megan to Taylor and back again, making her big puppy ears swing. Something was definitely wrong. Kiki stood up with her paws on Megan's shoulder, and stuffed her cold black nose firmly into Megan's ear. That always made her laugh.

Megan did laugh this time, too, and so did Taylor, but somehow they still sounded sad.

"I suppose at least we can send each other e-mails," Taylor said, reaching out to pet Kiki, and Megan nodded.

"And we can chat on the phone all the time." Megan laughed. "Mom said she thought they might have to get me my own cell phone, we talk to each other so much! It won't be the same as taking Kiki to the park with you, though."

Kiki stood on the bed, listening to them with her head to one side. Something was definitely going on.

"I'm going to miss her, too," Taylor agreed, tickling Kiki's ears. "You know, Mom still won't let me get a dog because she says we don't have the time to take care of one. Now I won't even be able to share Kiki with you. And she's growing so quickly. I probably won't recognize her soon."

Kiki wagged her tail delightedly as

Taylor made a big deal over her.

"I'll e-mail you tons of photos," Megan promised. "And you're coming to stay over. Mom and Dad are going to get me a sleepover bed that slides under mine. Kiki can be half your dog again then."

"You'd better record her bark for me, too," Taylor reminded her. "I'll never get out of the house for school in the morning without Kiki barking outside the gate."

Kiki yawned. Megan and Taylor kept fiddling around with those boxes and talking, and no one was taking her for a walk. She was bored. She slid off the bed and squeezed underneath it. There were always interesting things to play with under there....

"I knew it!" Megan's dad put his head around the door five minutes later. "You two are sitting there chatting instead of filling boxes."

"We're sorry!" Megan and Taylor jumped up, and Megan grabbed a pair of sneakers and stuffed them quickly into a box, just to look busy.

"And what's Kiki doing under there?" Dad asked, peering around the end of Megan's bed.

Kiki crept out from under the bed looking rather guilty, with half a roll of brown packing tape attached to her whiskers. It was very chewy, though she didn't really like the taste, and it seemed to have stuck....

"Naughty Kiki!" Megan giggled. "I'm sorry, Dad. I'll clean her up…."

Dad shook his head. "Honestly, after she ate your mom's shoe yesterday, you'd think she'd have had enough of chewing things. Just keep an eye on her, okay?"

Megan nodded apologetically, and started to peel the tape off Kiki's muzzle. "Silly dog," she muttered lovingly as Kiki squirmed. "Yes, I know it's not nice, but you can't go around with packing tape all over you. There!"

After that the girls made a real effort with the packing, and for the next hour they hardly even chatted at all.

Kiki whined miserably. After Megan had taken the tape away and scolded her, she'd sat so patiently, waiting for someone to play with her, or take her for a walk, or at least pet her. But Megan and Taylor just kept taking things off the shelves and putting them into those strange-smelling boxes. Kiki didn't like it. This was her room, and it was changing. She liked it the way it was before.

"Oh, Kiki, are you bored?" Megan picked her up, hugging her gently. "I wish I could play with you, too. But we won't be much longer."

"Actually, I told Mom I'd be back around now," said Taylor, hugging Megan and Kiki both at the same time. "I can't believe you've only got tomorrow left!" She gulped. "I wish Mom hadn't arranged for us to go and see my cousins, not on your last day. Call me soon? Promise! 'Bye, Megan!" Then she dashed out of the room and down the stairs, almost slamming the front door behind her.

Megan sat down limply on her bed, looking around at the piles of boxes, all labeled by Taylor in her favorite glittery felt tip markers with her best spelling. "It's going to be wonderful," she told Kiki again, but this time she didn't feel quite so sure.

Chapter Two
In the Way

Packing up had been an adventure to start with, but by the second day, everyone was starting to get grumpy.

It was such a huge job. The moving truck was coming early the next morning, and everything had to be packed up by then. Megan could tell that her mom was panicking that they wouldn't be ready in time.

She was trying to stay out of the way as much as possible, but it wasn't easy with Kiki. Mom and Dad were much too busy to take her for a walk, and Megan wasn't allowed to go out on her own, so Kiki was full of energy, and she couldn't burn it off. Already that morning she'd chewed a roll of bubble wrap into tiny pieces all over the living room floor, and she kept managing to be in everyone's way.

"Mom, stop!" Megan yelled as her mom lowered a box of books onto the hall floor.

"What? What is it?" Her mom straightened up, red-faced with effort, and peered worriedly over the top of the huge box.

"You were just about to squish Kiki

with that!" Megan helped her mom put the box down on top of another one, then pointed to the space she'd been aiming for. Kiki was sitting there, wagging her tail and looking very pleased with herself.

Mom sighed. "You're going to have to take her into the yard. I'm sorry, Megan, but Kiki's going to get hurt if she stays in here. She's better off outside."

"Come on, Kiki!" Megan tried to sound enthusiastic as she led Kiki out into the yard. She'd found the red-and-white-striped knotted rope toy that Taylor had given Kiki for Christmas in her basket, so at least they could play.

Kiki loved racing up and down the yard after the rope—it was her favorite toy—although she didn't see why she

always had to give it back to Megan
after she'd fetched it. It was much more
fun to chew it to pieces. She shook her
head vigorously as Megan tugged at the
toy, laughing.

"Give it to me, you silly girl! I'm
going to throw it again!"

"Megan, can you come here a minute?" It was Mom, calling from inside. With everyone already a little grumpy, she knew she'd better go and see what Mom wanted, rather than pretend she hadn't heard.

"I'll be back in a minute," she promised Kiki and dashed inside.

Kiki shook the toy a few more times and growled at it in case it was thinking of fighting back. At last she dropped it on the grass, nosing it hopefully. Where was Megan? This game wasn't as much fun without her. Kiki left the toy and trotted across the yard to the back door.

The door was closed, but Kiki scrambled up the back step anyway. The door didn't always shut properly,

and sometimes she could open it, if she nudged it hard with her nose at just the right place. Kiki pushed at the door. She wagged her tail proudly as it swung open, and she trotted inside.

Kiki wandered along the hallway, listening for Megan. Ah! That was her voice, coming from upstairs. She bounded up the stairs to find her.

Unfortunately, Megan's dad was coming down the stairs, with his arms full of pictures from the bedrooms that he needed to wrap in packing paper.

Kiki yowled as he accidentally stepped on her paw, and tried to shoot off through his legs.

Megan's dad stumbled down the stairs, twisting his ankle. He landed painfully at the bottom.

Clutching his ankle, he looked up to see Kiki staring down at him.

"Oh, that dog!" he yelled. "Megan! Kiki just tripped me up on the stairs. You're supposed to be watching her! I thought Mom told you to put her outside."

Megan and her mom had heard the crash, and they were already running along the landing.

"She didn't mean to!" Megan protested, hurrying to pick up Kiki, who was whimpering in fright. "I'm sorry, Dad, she *was* outside. I guess I didn't shut the back door all the way. It wasn't her fault. Are you okay?"

"No," her father muttered angrily, rubbing his ankle. "Take that dog outside, now. Ow!"

Megan carried Kiki back into the yard. The little dog was shivering. She wasn't used to being shouted at, and she'd never heard Megan's dad sound so mad. Megan sat down on the bench and cuddled Kiki, whispering soothing words. "Shhh, he didn't mean it. I'm sorry, Kiki. I should have made sure you couldn't get back in."

Kiki snuggled into her fleecy top, still shaking. At least Megan wasn't angry with her. She whined with pleasure as Megan rubbed her ears.

She knew Megan would always be there to take care of her.

Chapter Three
A Confusing Change

Kiki rested her chin on Megan's shoulder as she lovingly rubbed her head over and over.

"Megan!" Mom was calling from inside. Megan stood up slowly, carrying Kiki. She was growing so fast! She had been so small when they got her, and it had been easy to hold her like this. But now she was getting heavier.

"Oof, Kiki, my arms are going to fall off," Megan teased her lovingly as she carried her across the yard. She felt Kiki tense up a little as they went into the kitchen to join Mom and Dad. Obviously she remembered Dad shouting at her. "Hey, shh, it's okay," she whispered. But Kiki buried her nose in Megan's neck and whimpered.

"Is Kiki all right?" Mom asked. "She didn't get hurt, too, did she?"

Megan shook her head. "No, I think she's just upset. She didn't know what was going on. I'm really sorry she tripped you up, Dad. How's your ankle?"

Dad had it propped up on the chair in front of him, covered by a bag of frozen peas. "I'll live. But this has made us think, Megan. Mom and I have talked it over, and we're sure it's the right thing to do now...."

"What is?" Megan asked cautiously. From the way Mom and Dad were looking, she had a feeling it was going to be something she wouldn't like.

"Kiki's really been getting in the way while we've been packing, Megan," Mom explained. "It's going to be the same when the movers are loading up, and when we're unpacking at the new house, too. It's just not practical having a puppy around. Dad could have been hurt really badly."

"She didn't mean to," Megan pleaded. "She's only little. She wasn't trying to be naughty."

"We know that, but we're so busy, and no one has the time to exercise Kiki properly right now. So she's even bouncier and sillier than usual! Aren't you?" Dad reached out very gently to pet the puppy. "Oh, my, I really did scare her," he said sadly, as he saw Kiki's eyes widen nervously as he came close. "It isn't fair to her."

Megan gulped. She could see that they were right—she could hardly argue that Kiki wasn't getting in the way, when Dad was sitting there with a hurt ankle. "But what are you going to do?" she whispered. "You're not going to make us give her back to Mrs. Johnston, are you?" Mrs. Johnston was the owner of the rescue center where they had gotten Kiki. She felt tears starting to well up in her eyes. "Please don't say we have to give her back!" she choked out. "It wasn't her fault! I'll be more careful, I promise!"

"Megan, Megan, calm down! Of course we're not sending Kiki back." Mom laughed, hugging her and Kiki. "This is only for a few days while we move. We don't want to get rid of Kiki, but when we first started planning the move, your grandma said she could help out and take Kiki for a while if we needed her to. So I called Grandma just now, and she said she'd love to have her. She'll drive up and get Kiki and take her back to her house until we've settled in, just for a couple of days. We'll pick her up on Tuesday."

"We're all going to be so busy, you'll hardly notice she's gone," Dad said encouragingly.

Megan held Kiki tightly, feeling the warm weight in her arms. She didn't want to send Kiki away. Not when she was already upset. She was sure Kiki would hate it.

"She won't understand," she said sadly. "I know she loves Grandma, but she's never stayed with her. She's never stayed anywhere without me! She'll think I've abandoned her.... She's really confused with all the packing already, and she doesn't understand what's going on. Couldn't I just be really, really careful and keep her in the yard and not let her get in the way?" Megan begged. "I know Grandma will take care of her, but Kiki's used to having me. She'll be miserable somewhere else. And Grandma has a cat—that's not going to work! Sid will hate having Kiki in the house!"

Megan looked down at the puppy. Kiki liked chasing cats....

"I'm sure your grandma will figure

something out," Dad said, smiling. "Sid and Kiki will probably be curled up on the couch together by the time we go and pick Kiki up."

Megan shook her head disbelievingly. "Please...?" she whispered.

Mom sighed. "I'm sorry, Megan. We've already had one accident. And I almost squashed Kiki with that box this morning. This just isn't the right place for a puppy right now. And the new house, too. We don't really know what it's like—there might be all kinds of places where she could get herself into trouble. We need to check everything out first to make sure she's safe."

Kiki gave an anxious little whine. She could feel that Megan wasn't happy, and she didn't like it. She licked Megan's cheek lovingly and looked at her with big, worried eyes.

Megan pressed her cheek gently against Kiki's soft ears. It wasn't just Kiki who was going to hate this. Megan had been counting on having Kiki to cheer her up over the next couple of days. It was going to be so hard to leave her old home and her best friend. And now it looked like she was going to have to do it all on her own.

Grandma drove up from Westbury later that afternoon to pick Kiki up. Kiki had a special dog cage for traveling, and it barely fit on the back seat of Grandma's car. Megan carefully packed up Kiki's basket and blanket, and her bowls and food—including her favorite bone-shaped biscuits. Then there was a bagful of toys, her leash, her blanket—the list went on and on.

"My goodness!" Grandma muttered. "How many dogs am I taking care of?"

"Thanks so much for doing this," said Megan's mom. "It's a huge help."

Kiki was trotting backward and forward after Megan as she carried all her things to make a pile in the hall. She was very confused about what was going on, but she'd seen Megan's dad moving her travel cage into Grandma's car, so she thought she and Megan must be going somewhere with Grandma. They had driven out for special walks in the woods with her before. It must be that—although Kiki didn't see why she would need her basket and everything else just to go out for the day.

"Okay." Grandma finished her cup of

tea. "We'd better be off then, if we don't want to get back too late. We'll see you all on Tuesday." She hugged Megan. "Oh, I'm so excited about having you all living so close. It's going to be wonderful."

Megan hugged her back. She was excited, too, but she couldn't help worrying about Kiki. "Grandma, you'll make sure she's not lonely tonight, right? She usually sleeps on my bed," she reminded her anxiously.

"I'll do my best," Grandma promised. "I think Sid would leave home if a dog came and tried to sleep on my bed with him, but how about I give Kiki a hot-water bottle to cuddle up next to?"

Megan nodded sadly as she pictured Kiki spending the night on her own.

"It's only for two days, Megan," Dad said, putting an arm around her shoulders. "Kiki will be fine."

Kiki hopped into her cage happily enough, expecting Megan to come and sit next to her in the back. She would probably waggle her fingers through the door and tickle her ears.

But Grandma was getting into the car without Megan. Kiki looked around anxiously and barked to tell her she'd made a mistake. Grandma looked back over her shoulder and smiled. "It's all right, Kiki. Shhh. Don't worry. We'll see Megan again soon."

Kiki stared back at her. Yes, *Megan*. Grandma must know what was wrong. Why were they going without Megan? She felt the vibrations and howled in despair as Grandma started the car. Megan was being left behind! Kiki stood up on her hind legs in the cage, trying to look out the window, but she could only see the side of the car and Grandma's seat in front.

Megan was clinging to her mom's arm, trying to stop herself from racing after Kiki and yelling at Grandma to stop the car. "Oh, Mom, listen to her howling," she said miserably. "She's so upset. Does she really have to go to Grandma's?"

Her mom just hugged her.

Kiki couldn't see Megan, but she could hear her, and she sounded unhappy. She scratched frantically at the bars of her cage with her paws, desperate to get back to Megan.

As the car pulled away down the road, Kiki barked and barked.

At last, when it hurt to bark anymore, she stopped. She pressed her nose against the door of the travel cage.

Grandma had taken her away from Megan, and Megan hadn't wanted her to go. Of course she hadn't! Kiki was Megan's dog. Kiki didn't understand what was going on, but she was absolutely certain about one thing.

She had to get back to Megan.

At Grandma's house, everything smelled different. Kiki had been there before, but only with Megan, when it had been fun. Grandma was doing her best—she'd taken Kiki for a walk when they first arrived to stretch her legs after being in the car. But Kiki had trailed along behind her with her ears drooping, and in the end, Grandma had turned back.

But it was worse in the house. Kiki didn't want to be here, and she *hated* cats. Sid was huge and black and old, and very grumpy. He didn't like dogs at all, and he really didn't like dogs who barked and jumped around all over the place. He stood on the back of an armchair and hissed angrily when he first saw Kiki. With all his fur standing up like that and his tail fluffed up like a brush, Sid was almost as big as she was.

Grandma carefully made sure they were kept apart after that, shutting Kiki in the kitchen. But then the phone rang, and she forgot to close the kitchen door when she came out to the hall to answer it. Kiki trotted out after her—she might not want to be here, but Grandma was her one link with Megan.

Sid was sitting in the middle of the hallway like a furry black rock.

Kiki bounced at him bravely and barked, but Sid shot forward and scraped his claws across her nose. Kiki yelped. She'd chased cats before, or tried to, anyway—Megan didn't like her chasing things. But the cats had never fought back before. She stared at Sid worriedly, and he hissed again. It was a clear warning.

Kiki crept behind the couch and stayed there, sulking, until Grandma tempted her out with a handful of bone-shaped biscuits, the ones that Megan always gave her. Even those just made her miss Megan more. Grandma took her back into the kitchen away from Sid and tried to give her lots of attention, but Kiki didn't really want to play. She was too confused.

Maybe Megan would come and get her soon. She had been here with Megan before, after all. And she definitely remembered Sid, and the way this house smelled so strongly of cat. Megan must be coming later, Kiki decided hopefully. Every time footsteps went past on the sidewalk outside, she pricked up her ears and wagged her tail. But as the afternoon wore on, she stopped bothering. It never was Megan, and now it was getting dark.

She padded over to her basket and stared at it miserably. If Megan was coming to get her, she wouldn't need her basket. Her food bowls were here, too, and her toys. Why would they be here if Megan was coming to take her home?

"Can I talk to Kiki, Grandma?" Megan asked, gripping the phone tightly.

"I'm not sure that's a very good idea, Megan," Grandma said gently. "It might upset her. She'll be fine. I'm going to put a hot-water bottle in her basket, and she's got her blanket and all her usual things. I'm sure she'll have settled down by the morning."

Which means she isn't settled down now, Megan thought unhappily as she said good-bye. Kiki was hating being at Grandma's, just as Megan had thought she would.

They were having take-out for dinner, as a treat, so they didn't have to cook, but Megan hardly ate anything.

It wasn't the same without Kiki lurking hopefully under the table in case anyone dropped a tasty morsel.

She was feeling so miserable that she went to bed early, but it took her a long time to get to sleep—her room was full of boxes, and they all looked strange and gloomy in the dark. *Only until Tuesday*, Megan told herself. *Today is Sunday. By Tuesday afternoon, I'll have Kiki back.*

That night, Kiki was left alone in Grandma's kitchen. She had her own familiar basket and her blanket, which was wrapped around a cozy hot-water bottle, but she was still desperately homesick.

She whined unhappily for a long while, but Grandma didn't come down. Kiki was tired, but her basket felt wrong with the hot-water bottle in it. It had cooled down now, and it sloshed and wobbled when she moved. Kiki tried to push it out, but it was heavy, so she picked it up in her teeth and tried to drag it instead. Still it wouldn't budge. She tugged again, and the water started to leak out all over her blanket.

Kiki howled. Why had Megan abandoned her?

Chapter Four
Escaping Grandma's

Kiki woke up in her damp basket. She eyed the hot-water bottle worriedly. People didn't like it when she chewed things. She looked up anxiously as the kitchen door opened, wondering if Grandma would be very angry.

But she only laughed. "Oh, dear, they did say you liked chewing things at the moment. It's all right, Kiki. I know you didn't mean to be naughty. It was probably silly of me to let you have it. I just didn't think. Don't be sad, little one—you'll see Megan again soon."

Kiki stared up at Grandma with mournful eyes, as she cleaned up her damp things. Even though Grandma was being friendly, she didn't want to stay here. If only she could go back home to Megan.

Kiki was good at finding things, and she was best at finding Megan. She smelled special, and Kiki could always find her. She knew when Megan was coming home from school—she could just feel it. She somehow knew when it was time to go and sit by the door, so she could be there to see Megan as soon as she got inside.

So it would be no problem to find Megan, Kiki was sure. But finding her meant she had to get out first, and she wasn't sure about doing that.

Grandma fed Kiki, then let Sid into the kitchen to give him breakfast. After that, she left the door open so Kiki could get out of the kitchen, too. Grandma watched them anxiously, but this time, the cat and the puppy stayed out of each other's way.

After a while, Kiki crept out of the kitchen, watching carefully for Sid. She was fairly sure he was in his favorite place—on the back of the couch, so he could look out the window and see exactly what was going on in the street.

The front door was very big and very solid. It had a handle, which Kiki couldn't reach, even standing on her hind legs. The mail slot was at the bottom of the door, but even though she could get her claws into it to scratch it open, it was only big enough for her nose, and even that hurt. Kiki sat staring at the door hopelessly, then she gave her ears a determined shake. If she couldn't open it, she would just have to wait until someone opened it for her.

She hung around the hallway all morning, waiting for the door to be opened and half-playing with her squeaky fish toy.

She was just scrambling underneath a table, trying to reach the squeaky fish, when there was the shrill sound of the doorbell. Kiki jumped, banging her head on the bottom of the table.

She could hear someone shifting around on the doorstep. This was her chance!

Kiki wriggled herself out from under the table, so that her nose was sticking out, and watched as Grandma hurried to answer the door. It was the mail carrier with a package. Grandma opened the door wider to take the sheet of paper she needed to sign, and Kiki's ears pricked up as she saw what was beyond it. Grandma's house didn't have a fenced-in front yard like Megan's house did, just a flowerbed and then straight onto the sidewalk. As Grandma turned away from the door to rest the sheet of paper on the very table Kiki was hiding under, Kiki darted out the door.

Kiki's heart was thumping as she hid herself behind an enormous clump of striped leaves under the front window. She had expected the mail carrier to see her and shout, and maybe try to catch her, but he was too busy talking to Grandma. Still, Kiki was sure Grandma would see her if she tried to run down the street now. Hiding was best. She watched anxiously as Grandma gave the sheet back, and the door began to close. Was she going to notice?

Some strange sense made her look up just then, and she almost gave herself away with a yelp.

Sid was staring down at her from his perch on the back of the couch. He knew she was there. What if he meowed and Grandma discovered she'd gotten out?

Kiki watched Sid nervously. Should she run now, and see if she could get far enough away in the few seconds she had left? But Sid wasn't meowing to get Grandma's attention. He was sitting very still, just watching with disapproving eyes, the tip of his tail twitching very slightly.

The front door slammed shut. Kiki gulped. *He wasn't going to stop her.* She supposed it made sense. He didn't want her in his house any more than she wanted to be there. Kiki wagged her tail at him gratefully, then sneaked out from behind the bush and onto the sidewalk.

She needed to get away from Grandma's house fast, before Grandma realized what had happened and came to find her. Kiki looked around, her tail wagging very slightly. She couldn't help but be excited. She was heading back to Megan! She was going to find her, all by herself!

She was going home.

Kiki skittered quickly across the street, heading for a little side road with high bushes that led down between some of the houses. Grandma wouldn't see her here, she was sure.

Once she was on the side street, she raced as fast as she could. They had gone down here on the walk yesterday; it was leafy and overgrown, with lots of hiding places.

Finally she ran out of breath and collapsed, panting, underneath a tangle of brambles. She lay in the leafy dimness, breathing fast, and loving the feeling of being out on her own. Walks with Megan were the best thing, of course, but it was fun not to have a leash on and to be able to go where she liked. The bramble bush smelled nice. Earthy, but sweet at the same time.

Kiki tried to figure out which way she should go next. Where was Megan? Which way?

She rested her nose on her paws. It wasn't that she was going to sniff Megan out exactly—that would be silly, as she was too far away for that. This was different from finding Megan's scent. It was more of a feel. Megan—and home—was that way.

Kiki wriggled eagerly out from under the brambles and set off down the side street. She knew it was going to be a long way—longer than any walk she'd done before—but she wasn't scared. She was Megan's dog, not Grandma's, and she was meant to be with Megan.

Back at the house, Grandma was searching anxiously for Kiki. She hadn't missed her until a few minutes ago, when she had put out Kiki's lunch and she hadn't come running. She was hoping that the puppy was hiding in the house somewhere.

"Kiki! Here, girl! Where are you?"

Grandma crouched down to check behind the couch, in case Sid had frightened her again and Kiki had tucked herself away. The cat was still curled up on the back of the couch.

"Where can she be, Sid?" Grandma muttered worriedly. "Oh, she didn't get out when the mail carrier came, did she? I would have seen her, I'm sure. And that's the only time I've opened the door all day. But then where has she gone? I've looked everywhere."

Grandma thought sadly about Megan—they'd be leaving their old house right about now, she expected. Megan would be so excited; how could she spoil their moving day by telling them Kiki was lost? But if she didn't find the puppy soon, she would have to.

Sid followed as she went out into the hallway and opened the front door. Grandma looked up and down the street anxiously, while Sid coiled around her ankles, purring lovingly.

He really didn't like dogs in his house.

The small side street led out onto a main road. It was a busy road, and it didn't have wide sidewalks for people and dogs to walk on, like the ones Kiki was used to. She stood hesitating on the little patch of ground where the small street and the road met, and watched the cars whooshing past. She wasn't supposed to go near cars. She had been very carefully trained to sit and wait at the edge of the sidewalk until Megan said to walk.

Cautiously, Kiki stretched out one paw onto the road, then jumped back with a frightened yelp as a car shot by in a speeding rush of air. Kiki looked around and decided that she wouldn't cross, even though the small street continued on the other side of the road. She would walk along the edge of the main road instead. She was fairly sure she would still be going the right way. She set off, but the edge of the road was only a narrow fringe of dusty grass below the hedges. Every time a car went past it ruffled Kiki's fur, and the tires screeched and scared her. She kept jumping into the bushes in fright.

Kiki was cowering in a hedge, waiting for an enormous truck to thunder past, when she realized that just in front of her was a hole. It was a gap in the thick bush, leading away from this horrible, frightening road! Kiki darted through it and found herself in a field. This was much better. There were no cars, only long grass that was fun to run through. Kiki darted across the field happily. This was definitely the best way to go—no more roads, she decided, at least until she got close to Megan's house, where there were roads all around.

Kiki reached a line of hedges leading to the next field and nosed along it, looking for a good place to scramble through. It was thick and prickly, but suddenly she found a small tunnel. Kiki wriggled into it—then stopped.

She was stuck! Her collar had gotten caught on something. She pulled frantically, but the collar only tightened around her neck until it hurt. She tried again, and again, but she couldn't break the collar, or the branch it had gotten caught on.

At last, worn out from pulling, she sat still, whimpering a little. Something else must use this tunnel, and she didn't want to be here when it came back. Pulling at the collar just wasn't going to work—but when Megan had first put it on her, she had managed to get it off, hadn't she? It had been a little big and it wasn't now, but maybe if she really tried.... Instead of pulling forward, Kiki wriggled backward, twisting her neck so that she reversed out of her collar, wrenching it over her ears.

Kiki fell backward, rolling over in the leaves. She had done it! Her ears felt like she had half pulled them off, but although her collar was still stuck in the bush, she wasn't. Kiki stepped out into the next field, her legs shaky with relief.

The next bush was easy; she edged through it on her tummy and hardly even caught her fur. But as she wriggled through she could smell something strange on the other side.... The field she came out in was full of cows. Kiki had only ever seen cows at a distance, and she'd never walked through a field full of them. They were very large. She stood watching for a moment, but the cows didn't seem to notice her. Most of them were grazing, although a few were lying down quietly.

She took a cautious step out into the field, then started to trot quickly across it, keeping herself low to the ground and hoping the cows wouldn't notice her. The problem was that they were scattered everywhere, so she had to go close to a few of them. Luckily, she scampered past so quickly that they hardly had time to turn their huge heads before she'd left them behind. But a few of them got nervously to their feet at the sight of the dog.

Kiki was almost at the far edge of the field when she heard a heavy, lumbering tread behind her. She darted a look over her shoulder, her heart suddenly racing at double speed. An enormous black-and-white cow was thundering toward her, head lowered to show off short but business-like horns. It was staring angrily straight at Kiki, and it snorted at her in fury.

Kiki ran faster than she ever had before, racing at top speed for the hedge. She could feel the cow's hot breath as it huffed behind her. Its enormous hooves trampled the grass, inches away from her tail. Kiki let out a frightened bark. She had to go faster!

Chapter Five
On the Run!

Megan stood in her bedroom, surrounded by boxes. It felt so strange that she had been doing just the same thing a couple of hours ago, but in her old house. There her room had looked really sad, like the end of something, but here it was a new start. It was so exciting! She just wished she had Kiki here to see everything, too. She peered

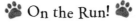

out her window at the big yard, sloping down to a stream, and the woods on the other side. Tomorrow she could go and explore it all with Kiki!

Megan was suddenly desperate to talk to Grandma and find out if Kiki was okay. She hurried downstairs.

"Dad, can I borrow your cell phone?" Megan asked, bursting into the kitchen.

But Dad was already on the phone, looking anxious.

Megan made an "I'm sorry!" face, but Dad only smiled at her distractedly.

"What's the matter?" Megan asked. Even the air in the kitchen felt full of worry.

"It's Grandma on the phone," Mom said quietly, putting her arm around Megan. "She called to say that she thinks Kiki slipped out the door this morning. But she's sure Kiki couldn't have gotten far."

"But, but—where could she have gone?" Megan asked in a frightened whisper. "She hardly knows anywhere around there. She'll get lost!"

Megan sat down at the table, feeling sick. She would never have let Kiki go if she'd thought this might happen. How could Grandma have let her get out?

Dad ended the call, then sat down next to her and covered her hand with his. "Grandma's going to come over and pick you up so you can go and look for Kiki with her."

Megan nodded, feeling a little bit better. But it was so hard to think of Kiki, lost and lonely and scared. She had to try very hard not to cry.

Grandma hugged her when she arrived, and she looked so upset that Megan forgot to be angry and just hugged her back.

"We'll find her, Megan," she promised. "I'm so sorry. She must have slipped out when the mail carrier came. I just didn't see. She's probably off exploring in the woods. The moment she hears your voice, she's sure to come running."

They drove back to Grandma's, and then set off into the woods that ran behind the houses, calling and calling.

But Kiki didn't come running, as Megan had so hoped she would. The daffodils were flowering and it was really beautiful—Megan had been looking forward to walking here with her dog so much. But all she could think about now was how scared Kiki would be out here on her own. She was still tiny, and most of their walks were in the park. Kiki could get trapped in a rabbit hole, or fall in a stream! Megan sniffed hard and rubbed her sleeve across her eyes.

"Let's go and search the side street,"

Grandma suggested, looking around one last time. "I just don't think she can be here, because she would have heard us calling."

They found no sign of Kiki on the side street, either. They went all the way down to the road, and Megan watched the cars speeding by. What if Kiki had been run over? She had tried so hard to teach her to be careful, but she was only a puppy, and she might easily have run into the road.

"I don't think she'd come along here," Grandma said, hugging her. "Don't worry, Megan. Kiki would be frightened of those cars if she was on her own. She wouldn't try to cross. Come on, let's go back home. I've already asked my neighbors, but we'll go and ask around town if anyone has seen her. Someone must have, I'm sure."

But Grandma looked worried. It was as though Kiki had simply disappeared.

Kiki made a big leap and shot into the hedge, the cow snorting angrily behind her. It lowered its horns, as Kiki fought and scrambled her way through the twigs. She gave a yelp of relief as she struggled out into tufts of long grass on the other side of the hedge.

The cow snorted grumpily and lumbered away, and Kiki collapsed panting on the soft grass. She'd left her collar in the last hedge, but it felt like she'd left half her fur in this one.

Now that she was safely away from the cows, Kiki realized how hungry she was, and thirsty, too. She hadn't had lunch, and it seemed like a long way past lunchtime now. But although the sun was sinking, it was still warm. The air felt sticky, and black clouds were gathering behind the trees.

The quiet road was leading to houses, just a few. *There might be some food around*, Kiki thought hopefully. And somewhere to rest. She didn't want to stay out in the open all night. She didn't like that strange close feeling in the air. It made her fur feel prickly.

"Mom called the vet just now and reported her missing." Megan gulped. "She's been gone all day, Taylor! The vet said it's good that she's microchipped, because if someone brings her in, they can check. Mom gave them our new address. Grandma and I searched and searched, and then we made posters on her computer. We've put them up everywhere, but no one has called. I wish you were here to help us look." Megan was sitting in her new bedroom, borrowing Dad's cell phone to call

Taylor. She hated having to tell her that Kiki was missing. It made it seem even more real.

"Oh, Megan!" Taylor sounded almost as upset as she was. "Have you been all through those woods you told me about?"

"We've searched the woods twice, and Mom says I can't go again now because it's getting dark," Megan said sadly. "I just want her back. She'll be so scared, Taylor. I hate thinking of her all on her own."

The first house Kiki came to had its garbage cans tightly closed. She headed on past. There was a good smell coming from somewhere close. *Bread,* she thought, sneaking carefully down the side of a house and squirming under an iron gate. *Yes!* There were bread crusts scattered all over a patio around a bird table. Kiki gobbled them greedily. She was so glad to find some food that she didn't notice she was being watched. The slam of a door made her jump back in fright. An elderly lady came out, looking angry and waving a broom. She poked it at Kiki, who skittered back in horror.

"Shoo! Out of here, you bad dog! Don't you scare away my birds! Shoo! Go home!" And she banged the brush on the patio stones, making Kiki squeak with fright. The puppy shot across the yard toward the gap under the gate, wriggling out and away as quickly as she could.

Once she was safely a few houses away, she hid under a car, shivering. She hadn't known the bread was special; she was just hungry. Kiki whimpered. She wanted Megan back. Then she shook her ears determinedly. She was on her way to Megan. She had a feeling that she had walked along this road before, with Megan and Grandma when they were out together. It was definitely the way home. She poked her nose out from under the car, checking for the elderly lady, but there was no one around.

It was getting dark, though. She wanted to keep going, but the stormy feeling in the air was getting stronger, and she could hear low growls of thunder. It made the fur stand up on her back. She would have to find somewhere to stop for the night. All of a sudden, the grayish sky split with a bright flash of lightning, and a heartbeat later, thunder crashed down. Kiki howled and dived through a gate into a front yard.

She raced into the yard, looking around desperately for somewhere to hide from those horrible noises. A house! A little wooden house, right here in the corner, just the right size for a dog. There were spotted curtains blowing in the window, and the door was open the tiniest crack. Kiki nosed at it, pushing it wider, and sneaked inside. There was even a cushion on the floor, along with a bunch of crayons. Kiki collapsed onto the cushion gratefully and closed her eyes. It seemed like a very long time since she'd run away that morning.

Soon Kiki was fast asleep.

A few miles away, Megan was lying awake. She wasn't really scared of thunder, not when she was safe inside. But tonight, it was terrifying. She kept imagining Kiki outside, frightened by the rumbling thunder. What if she was hurt? What if she was hiding under a tree to get out of the rain, and the tree was struck by lightning?

Megan watched the rain beating against the windows and shivered. It was a long time before she finally huddled under her blankets and drifted off into a troubled sleep.

The creak of the wooden door opening woke Kiki with a start. She shot upright, backing nervously into the corner of the playhouse.

A little boy was staring at her. He looked just as amazed as she did.

"A dog!" he breathed delightedly. "A dog's here!"

He sounded friendly, and Kiki relaxed a little, but she didn't go closer. Most children she met with Megan loved her and wanted to pet her, but Megan wouldn't let her jump up at children, or even sniff them. One little girl had seen her walking past, and then Kiki had gone to sniff her hand, and she'd squealed. Kiki had felt hurt. So now she watched this little boy carefully.

"Hello, dog...." He was crouching down now, staring into her eyes, and Kiki was sure that this one wasn't going to cry. "I'm Aiden. Did you come to stay? Are you going to live at my house?" He sounded very excited. "I know! You're hungry! Grandpa's dog is always hungry." He leaned closer and whispered, "Mommy's on the phone. I was having breakfast, but I came out when she wasn't looking. You can have my breakfast." He scrambled out of the little house and dashed away.

Kiki stood there blinking, not quite sure what was going on. She padded over to the door and peered out. Aiden was coming back, more slowly now, his dark head bent earnestly over a bowl.

"Here! My oatmeal. I've had enough, so you can finish it. And this is a bacon and egg sandwich. I don't like bacon, anyway."

Kiki could smell the bacon. After nothing but stale bread crusts since yesterday, it smelled like heaven. She trotted over to him and took it delicately from his hand as he held it out to her. It disappeared in about three bites.

"Wow, you are hungry." Aiden

sounded impressed.

Kiki sighed with pleasure, licking the bacon from around her whiskers, and looked hopefully at the bowl.

"Oh! Do you like oatmeal, too?" He put the bowl down on the ground for her and watched hopefully.

Kiki sniffed at it with interest. Oh, yes, she liked this. She gulped it down, licking the bowl thoroughly, then sat down, scratching her ear with one hind paw. She always did that after meals. It felt good.

Aiden laughed. "Funny dog," he said, crouching down to pet her gently.

Kiki closed her eyes and leaned against him happily. He reminded her of Megan, even though he was so little. She would see Megan soon—she just knew it!

"Oh!" Aiden straightened up. "Mom's calling me. I have to go. I'm going to ask her if you can stay! Mom! Mom!" He dashed back to the house, and Kiki watched the kitchen door swing shut behind him. She would have liked to stay with him for longer, but she was sure she wasn't that far from home now.

She crept past the playhouse and back under the front gate. She paused for a moment outside Aiden's house, to give him one last grateful bark, and then she went on her way.

Chapter Six
Homeward Bound

A few hours later, Kiki stood looking down into the river. She was sure she had just seen a fish. She had been here once before, one wonderful afternoon when they'd had a picnic, and Mom had scolded Megan for feeding her pieces of her sandwich. Remembering it made her feel hungry. She had walked a very long way since the bacon and egg sandwich.

Kiki set off again along the riverbank, wondering if she could catch a fish. That one had looked very slippery. And although she loved getting wet, she hadn't had a lot of practice swimming.

A-ha! Maybe this would be better than a fish. Just ahead of her, standing on the riverbank, was a man with a fishing rod, staring out over the water at his float. But what really interested Kiki was his bag of sandwiches, lying by his tackle box.

Kiki sneaked closer, and then darted out from behind a tree and seized a sandwich.

"Hey!" The fisherman shouted angrily, but he couldn't chase her without getting tangled in his line. He was trying to lay it down carefully, but Kiki didn't wait for him. Gripping the sandwich in her teeth, she ran for it, racing away down the overgrown path.

When his shouts died away into the distance, Kiki sat down to eat her prize: a tuna sandwich. So she was having fish after all!

She licked up the last crumbs from the grass and sighed happily. She felt much better now. She stood up and gave herself a brisk shake. It was time to set off for home again.

"Hello? Yes, this is Lindsey. Oh!" Mom beckoned frantically to Megan, who was listlessly picking at her dinner. She just didn't feel like eating—it made her worry about how hungry Kiki must be after a day and a half with no food.

"Who is it?" she asked, staring at Mom's excited face. Then she sat up straight, gasping. "Is it the posters? Has someone seen her?"

Mom was nodding. "Yes, yes, a Labrador puppy. Yes, very small. Let me write that down. By the bridge. Oh, dear, I am sorry. And that was this morning? Oh, thank you so much for calling us. Yes, I hope we will, too." She ended the call and turned to Megan, who was now standing right next to her, trying desperately to hear what the person on the other end of the line had been saying. "That was a man from town who was fishing down by Ellison Bridge this morning. Kiki stole his sandwiches!" Mom hugged her, laughing.

Megan smiled. "I was just thinking about how hungry she must be!"

"Come on, call your dad. Let's go and look for her. It's getting dark, but we should be able to see for a little while."

Kiki's paws were aching, but she felt so proud of herself. She had done it. She could see Megan's school playground, and the park was just around the next corner. She was so close! Despite her weariness, she trotted along faster. In a few minutes she would be back with Megan. She was just in time—already it was starting to get dark.

This was her street, and there was her house! Kiki looked carefully up and down the road for cars, then crossed over to her own front gate. She couldn't open it, but it was a pretty iron one that she could slip through, even though it was a tight fit. She stood outside the front door and barked happily. They were going to be so happy to see her!

No one came to the door, so she scratched at it with her front paws and barked again, louder and louder.

At last she heard footsteps. Kiki barked and jumped delightedly. She was going to see Megan!

But when the door opened, it wasn't Megan. Or even her mom or dad. There was a strange woman standing there, looking down at her in surprise.

Kiki whimpered, tucking her tail between her legs in confusion.

Megan was gone. She had left and abandoned Kiki with Grandma. Megan didn't want her anymore.

"What's going on?" A man was coming down the hall now, looking surprised. "Oh! A dog? Does it have a collar?"

"No, I don't think so." The woman bent down to look.

Kiki backed away from the doorstep miserably. She didn't know what to do. But the woman who'd answered the door followed her, talking gently. "Don't be scared, puppy. Are you lost? Oh, look, she's shivering, poor little thing. She's so pretty, and she can't be very old."

The man came out, too. "She must have slipped out of someone's house, don't you think? Maybe we'd better keep her for the night. We'll have to put her in the shed, though. Jasper would go crazy if we brought another dog in, and he's already upset about the new house. We can take her to the vet in the morning and see if she's been microchipped." And he reached down and scooped Kiki up.

The man carried Kiki around the side of her house, only it wasn't her house anymore, and she wasn't even allowed in. They put down a rug for her in the shed, with a bowl of water and some dog biscuits. It was comfortable, but she was in the yard and she was fenced in, when she should be inside, upstairs sleeping on Megan's bed.

Her family had gone away and left her. She just didn't understand. Even though Megan's dad had been angry with her, Megan had still cuddled her and talked to her and loved her the same way, hadn't she? Why had Megan left her behind? Had she just forgotten her?

Kiki buried her nose under her paws and whimpered. She'd spent so long trying to get home, and now home wasn't there.

Chapter Seven
Solving the Puzzle

Megan woke up and lay staring at the ceiling for a second. It looked wrong. Then she remembered she was in her new house. She felt a rush of excitement, until she looked down at the empty space at the end of her bed and remembered that Kiki was missing. She wished she could just go back to sleep and this would only be a dream.

She had been so hopeful yesterday evening when they'd gotten the phone call. They'd driven straight down to Ellison Bridge, which was on the way back to their old house. It was a beautiful place, and they'd taken Kiki there before for walks. She and Mom and Dad had searched all the way along the riverbank, calling, and banging Kiki's food bowl, something that the vet had suggested when Mom had spoken to her on the phone yesterday.

At last Dad had taken her hand. "Megan, it's getting dark. I think we have to stop."

"But we can't! She was here!" Megan had protested.

"We can come back in the morning and look again," Mom promised.

So Megan had to get up now. That man had definitely seen Kiki—there couldn't be two lost Labrador puppies, could there? She climbed out of bed wearily. She felt like she'd been dreaming about Kiki all night. In the worst dream, the puppy had been in the middle of the street, and Megan could hear a car coming. She shivered.

Megan started to pull on her robe, then suddenly she stopped and sat down on her bed again, staring wide-eyed at the photo on the shelf. It was a picture of her and Taylor and Kiki playing in their old yard. She reached over and picked it up. Why hadn't she figured it out sooner? Kiki had been at Ellison Bridge. Halfway back to their old house!

Kiki wasn't lost at all. She was trying to go home!

"Mom! Dad!" Megan went racing into their room. "Dad, where's your cell phone? We have to call the people at our old house. Kiki's gone home!"

Her parents were still half asleep, and her dad blinked at her wearily. "What do you mean?"

Megan sat down on the edge of the bed and started to explain. "She was really upset about being at Grandma's, wasn't she? She didn't understand what was going on. She doesn't know we've moved, Dad! She's trying to get back to our old house! She'd gotten halfway there yesterday morning. She's probably home by now!" Megan suddenly frowned. "Oh, no. She's going to find somebody else in our house." Her voice shook.

Mom sat up. "Megan, I don't think Kiki could have gotten that far. How could she find the way? It's a clever idea, but...."

"She got as far as Ellison Bridge!" Megan pointed out.

"Yes, I suppose so...."

"You do hear of dogs doing that kind of thing," Dad put in thoughtfully. "Maybe we should call the house, just in case. But it's too early right now."

Mom and Dad made her wait an entire hour before they called. Megan had walked in circles around the kitchen; she couldn't face breakfast. Now she was pressed close to Dad, trying to hear the phone conversation.

"She came to the door? Last night? No, we hadn't thought of calling you before, because it's such a long way. Almost 10 miles! That's wonderful. Yes, yes, of course, I see. I'm sure she would be fine in the shed. Yes, we'll come right away. We'll see you soon."

"They've found her!" Megan exclaimed. "They really have! Oh, Dad!" She was dancing now, jumping and flinging herself at her parents to hug them. Then she hurriedly put her boots on. They were going to get Kiki back!

🐾 🐾 🐾 🐾

Kiki lay on the rug in the chilly shed, wondering where she should go, now that she had no home anymore. She couldn't go back to Grandma's. Sid didn't like her, and she didn't want to live with him. She would have to find somewhere new.

The problem was, Kiki didn't want anywhere new. She only wanted Megan. But she certainly couldn't stay here. Kiki scrambled over the tangle of old garden equipment that was cluttering up the shed, sniffing out that fresh, cold breeze. There was a loose board in the wall! Kiki pushed it to one side and started to wriggle through. Her fur felt full of dust and splinters. She squeezed out the other side and shook herself briskly.

The new people had left the side gate open, and Kiki raced out down the side of the house. She didn't want them to close her in the shed again. She was about to run straight out of the front gate, but something stopped her.

Lying on the path, half-hidden by the garbage cans, was one of her toys. Her favorite toy. The red-and-white-striped knotted rope toy that Taylor had given her. Kiki picked it up in her teeth and shook it happily. It was so good to chew, and she loved it when Megan pulled the other end and then they'd play tug-of-war together.

Shaking the toy from side to side, Kiki knew, with sudden, happy certainty, that Megan had not left her behind. Not on purpose. Megan loved to play with her, and pet her, and talk to her.

Kiki trotted determinedly out of

her old front yard, squeezing quickly through the front gate, and set off down the street. She wasn't sure where she was going, but she was not going to give up. She reached the end of the street and looked around thoughtfully. She usually walked down here with Megan to pick up Taylor on her way to school.

Taylor! Taylor loved her, and she loved Megan. Taylor would know where Megan was! Kiki raced down the road, yelping with excitement, still carrying the rope toy.

As she turned the corner, she didn't notice a familiar car driving down the street. The car pulled up outside the house, and Megan leaped out. Without waiting for her parents, she went running up the path of their old house and rang and rang the doorbell.

Chapter Eight
Home at Last

Outside Taylor's front gate, Kiki dropped the rope toy and sat down proudly, just like she always used to. Then she barked loudly, three times.

She waited. She was just about to bark again when Taylor's front door opened, and Taylor rushed out onto the path.

"Kiki! I thought it was you barking, but Mom said it couldn't possibly be!

What are you doing here? Megan said on the phone last night someone had seen you at Ellison Bridge. How did you get all the way back here?" Taylor flung open the gate. "Oh, Kiki, we've all been so worried about you! Come on, Kiki, come! Here, girl!"

Taylor held the gate open wide and beckoned Kiki in.

Kiki picked up her toy and followed her. She trusted Taylor not to shut her in a shed. Taylor would help her get back to Megan, she was sure.

"Mom, Mom, look! Kiki's here! I told you it was her barking!" Taylor and Kiki dashed down the hall to Taylor's mom in the kitchen. "I have to call Megan, please, Mom?"

"Has she come all the way from

Megan's grandmother's house? She couldn't have! It must be at least 10 miles." Taylor's mom was staring at Kiki in amazement. "She doesn't have a collar—are you sure this is Kiki? You haven't just stolen someone's dog?"

"Mo-om! Of course it's Kiki! Look, she's carrying the toy that I bought her for Christmas. Besides, only Kiki would know to sit at the gate and bark three times. Oh, they're not answering." Taylor put down the phone with a crash and stared at Kiki. "Is it really 10 miles? How could she walk that far? And how did she know the way?"

"Well, dogs can be very clever," her mom said doubtfully. "But I don't know, to be honest. Because she was so desperate to find Megan, I guess."

Kiki barked, her eyes wide with hope. *Megan!* They had definitely said Megan.

"She heard you say it." Taylor laughed. "Are you trying to find Megan, Kiki?"

Kiki jumped up with her paws on Taylor's knees and barked and barked, wagging her tail frantically.

"It's okay. Megan will be here soon, I promise. She'll come and get you. Or we could take her to Megan's new house, couldn't we, Mom?"

Her mom frowned. "That might not be a good idea. She could get upset. Why don't we try calling the house again?"

Taylor nodded. "I have missed you, Kiki. But not as much as Megan has.

She's been searching for you all over the place." She rubbed Kiki's soft head. "She's going to be so happy to have you back."

Megan sat in the car outside her old house, gulping back tears. Her mom was sitting next to her, trying to calm her down, and her dad was leaning over from the front seat.

"I know it's hard, Megan, but I promise we'll find her. Come on, this is good news. We know she was here last night! That's a really good start."

Megan nodded, but she couldn't stop crying. "She came all this way to find us," she whispered tearfully. "And then there was someone else in her house. Another dog, too! She must have thought we just didn't love her anymore. What if she's gone off to find somewhere else to live?"

"I'm sure she didn't," Mom said firmly. "Kiki won't give up. She made it this far, didn't she? She'll be around here somewhere, probably just a little confused. Let's go and try the park."

But Kiki wasn't in the park, or on any of the streets around their old house. They called, Megan's dad whistled, and they stopped to ask everyone they saw. But there was no trace of her.

"She's gone." Megan had stopped crying now. She was almost too upset to cry. "We had our chance, and now we've lost her forever."

"Megan!" Her mom crouched down and hugged her. "I never thought I'd hear you giving up. You have to keep going—Kiki needs you to find her."

Megan nodded, biting her lip. Her mom was right. Kiki wouldn't give up on her, would she? "Can we go and see Taylor? Get her to look for Kiki? She won't know Kiki's back here, and she could ask people from school if she sees them."

"Good idea," her mom said. "Let's go back to the car—we'll drive over."

Megan rang Taylor's doorbell, thinking back to the last time she'd done that—on the final day of school, when Taylor had been running so late she hadn't come out of the house when Kiki barked. She'd been pulling on her coat when she opened the door, and she'd had a piece of toast sticking out of her mouth. She'd fed a little bit of it to Kiki.

Megan blinked. Why could she hear barking coming from inside Taylor's house? She didn't have a dog....

Just then, the door flew open. "I knew it! Did you get my message? I've called about six times! Why didn't you call me back?" Taylor's words were falling over each other in excitement, but Megan hardly heard her.

She was hugging Kiki—Kiki who'd leaped into her arms as soon as Taylor opened the door. The puppy's paws were on Megan's shoulders in a golden furry hug, and she was licking Megan's face all over.

Megan's parents laughed delightedly, and Taylor's mom started telling them about Kiki's sudden appearance.

Megan beamed at Taylor. "We didn't get any message because we weren't home. The people from the new house had found Kiki, but she slipped out of the shed. They had to put her in there because they had a dog, too, so—ugh, Kiki, don't lick my mouth! So they put

Kiki in their shed, but there's a hole in the shed wall, and she got out. She must have decided to come to you because she knows you really love her. Taylor, you found her!" And she hugged Taylor, too, squishing Kiki in between them.

"No, she found me," Taylor giggled. "She turned up and barked outside the gate. I thought I was dreaming!"

"Oh, Kiki, I'm never letting you go anywhere again," Megan gasped in between licks. "You're such a clever, wonderful dog—how did you find your way back here?"

Kiki sighed deeply and laid her chin on Megan's shoulder. All of a sudden, she felt very, very tired.

It had been a long journey, but now, at last, she was back home with Megan.

HOLLY WEBB

Holly Webb started out as a children's book editor, and wrote her first series for the publisher she worked for. She has been writing ever since, with more than 100 books to her name. Holly lives in England with her husband, three young sons, and several cats who are always nosing around when she is trying to type on her laptop.

For more information
about Holly Webb visit:

www.holly-webb.com
www.tigertalesbooks.com